TAM'S SLIPPER

First-Start® Legends

TAM'S SLIPPER

A STORY FROM VIETNAM

Retold by Janet Palazzo-Craig
Illustrated by Makiko Nagano

Troll

long time ago, a poor farmer
lived with his wife and his daughter,
Tam. But the farmer's wife died. He
soon married another woman. She
treated Tam badly.

Tam's father and his new wife had a baby girl named Cam. Now the stepmother made Tam work day and night. And to make things worse, Tam's father grew sick and died.

Each night, Tam slept in a dirty corner of the kitchen. She often dreamed wonderful dreams. In them, she wore fine clothes and married a prince.

Tam once asked her stepmother, "Why must I do all the work?"

"Spoiled child!" said the woman. "Who else will do it?"

One day, Cam and Tam went to the pond to catch prawns for dinner. Tam caught many, while Cam sat doing nothing.

When it was time to go home, Cam said, "Tam, would you get me that pretty flower across the pond?"

When Tam turned to get the flower, Cam quickly took the prawns and ran home. Tam sat down and cried.

Suddenly, someone said, "A princess should not cry." There stood a beautiful woman dressed in the royal colors of yellow and orange. "Tam, you are strong and kind. Someday you will be rewarded."

When Tam looked in her basket, a yellow and orange fish swam there. Tam put the fish in the pond. Each day she went to feed it.

One morning, Tam saw a rooster with shiny yellow and orange feathers. "Are you a royal rooster?" Tam teased. Then she fed the rooster from her own bowl.

Later, Tam took the cart to the fields. The horse seemed very hungry. Tam let it stop often to eat the grass. She saw how the horse's coat shone yellow and orange in the sun.

Later, Tam took the cart to the fields. The horse seemed very hungry. Tam let it stop often to eat the grass. She saw how the horse's coat shone yellow and orange in the sun.

Looking at the fields, Tam knew it would soon be time for the harvest festival. The prince would pay a visit to the village celebration.

On the day of the festival, the stepmother said, "Tam, you may go to the festival, but only after you have husked all the rice in this cart."

The rice was piled high! How could she ever finish such a task?

Just then, a flock of birds swooped down on the cart. Soon, every bit of rice was husked.

Then Tam saw a beautiful yellow blouse. She put it on. When she looked at herself in the pond, her special fish splashed her. Tam's ragged pants magically turned into new ones!

Next, Tam saw the rooster scratching in the dirt. It soon uncovered a pair of yellow and orange slippers. Tam put them on.

The horse appeared wearing a jeweled saddle. The beautiful woman that Tam had seen at the pond held the horse's reins. "You truly are a princess," she said.

As Tam rode the horse to the festival,
one of her slippers fell to the ground.

Later, the prince found the slipper. He had never seen one so beautiful. He called together all the women to find out who had lost the slipper.

Many tried, but it would fit no one. At last, Tam tried. It fit her perfectly!

In time, Tam and the prince fell in love and were married.

Day after day, the stepmother angrily scolded Cam, "Why didn't *your* foot fit in the slipper?" And day after day, the stepmother heard the sound of happy laughter that came from the prince and his bride. Tam's dream had come true!

 The story of *Tam's Slipper* comes from the country of Vietnam. Many cultures throughout the world have folktales and legends similar to this one. For example, in Europe, *Cinderella* is a popular story. It also tells of a kindly but poor and mistreated girl who dreams of a better life.